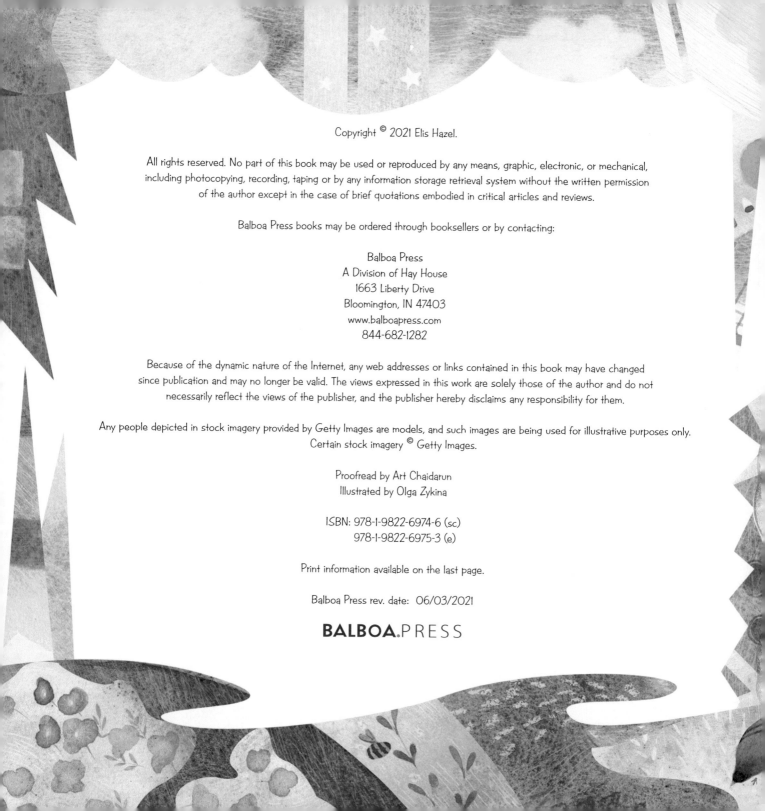

Balboa Press books may be ordered through booksellers or by contacting:

Balboa Press
A Division of Hay House
1663 Liberty Drive
Bloomington, IN 47403
www.balboapress.com
844-682-1282

Proofread by Art Chaidarun
Illustrated by Olga Zykina

ISBN: 978-1-9822-6974-6 (sc)
978-1-9822-6975-3 (e)

Print information available on the last page.

Balboa Press rev. date: 06/03/2021

BALBOA.PRESS

WHAT MEG LIKES TO LEARN

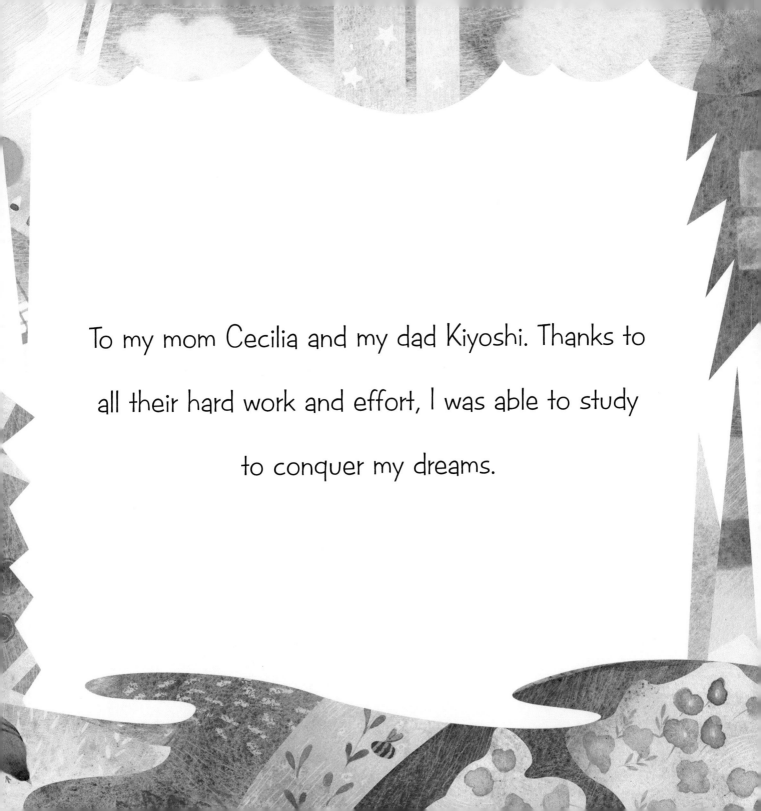

To my mom Cecilia and my dad Kiyoshi. Thanks to all their hard work and effort, I was able to study to conquer my dreams.

Every morning I like to go to school because

I meet my friends and I play with them.

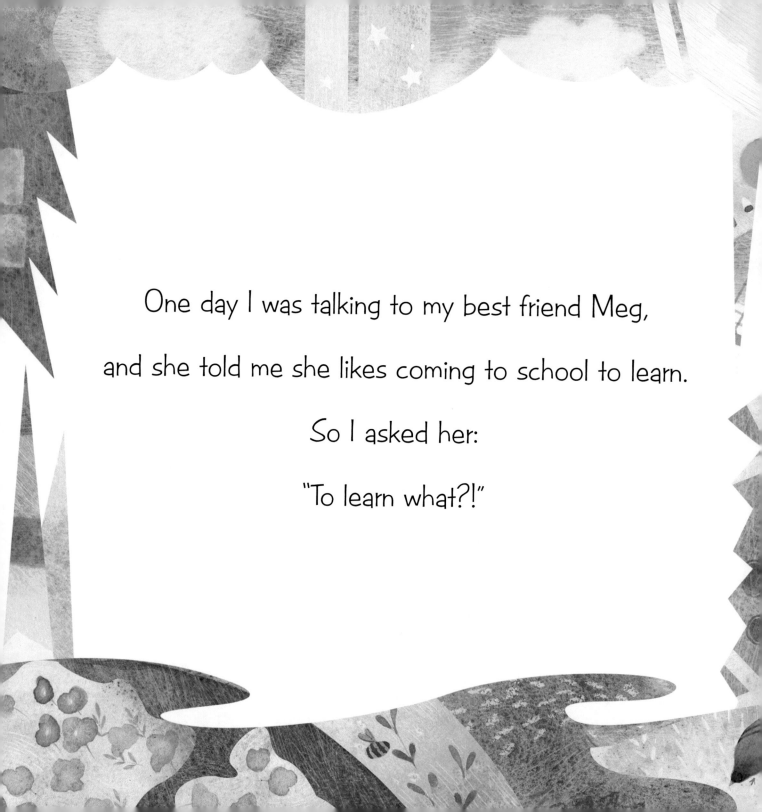

One day I was talking to my best friend Meg,

and she told me she likes coming to school to learn.

So I asked her:

"To learn what?!"

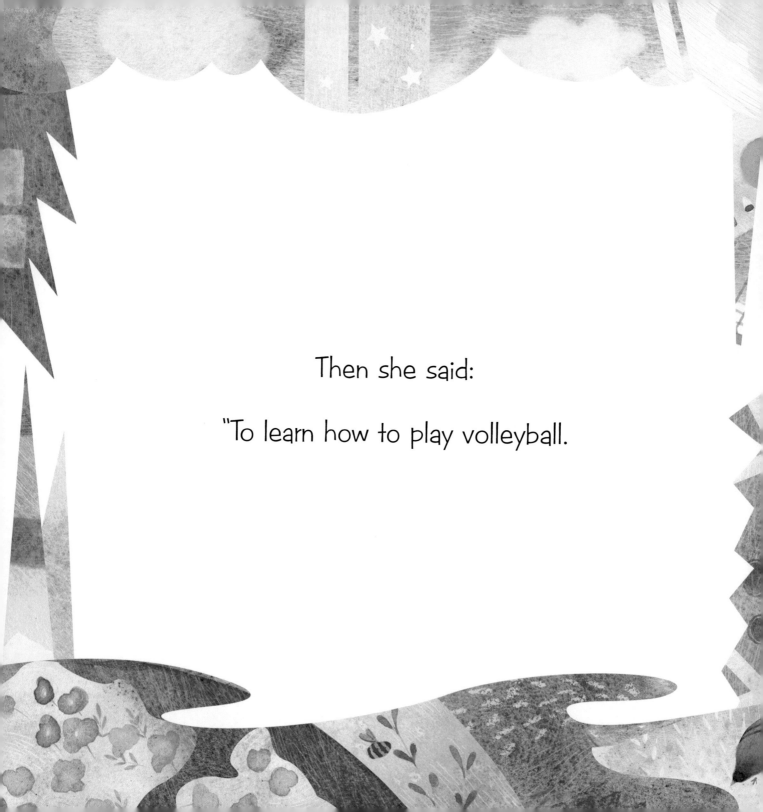

Then she said:

"To learn how to play volleyball.

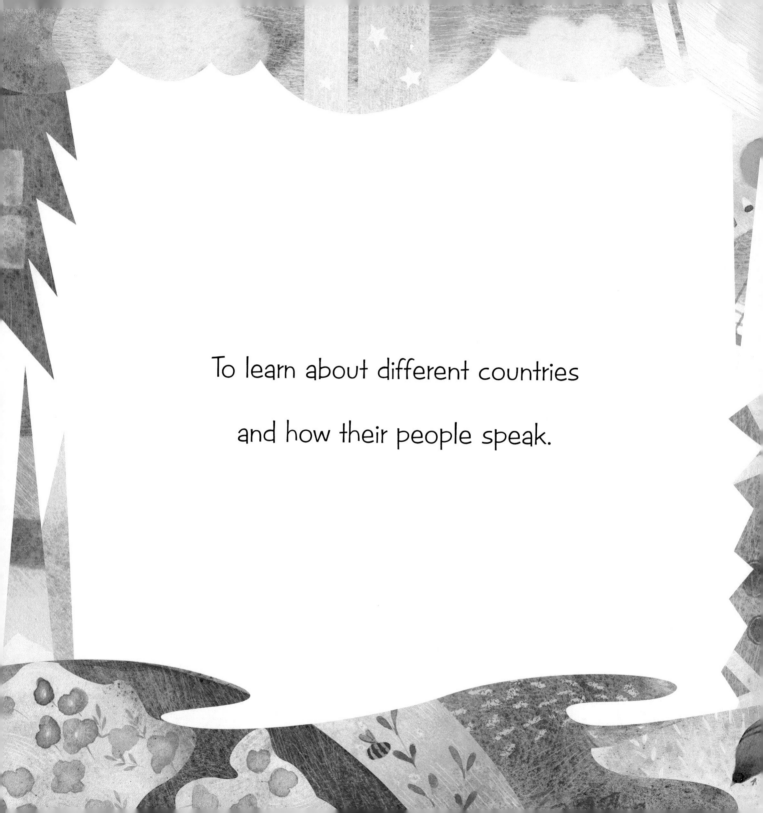

To learn about different countries

and how their people speak.

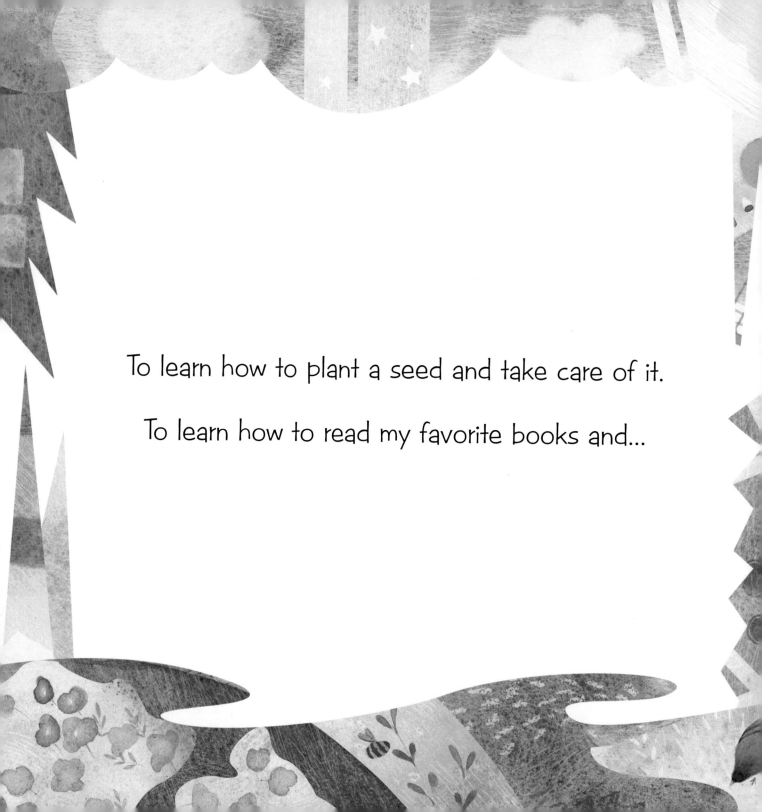

To learn how to plant a seed and take care of it.

To learn how to read my favorite books and...

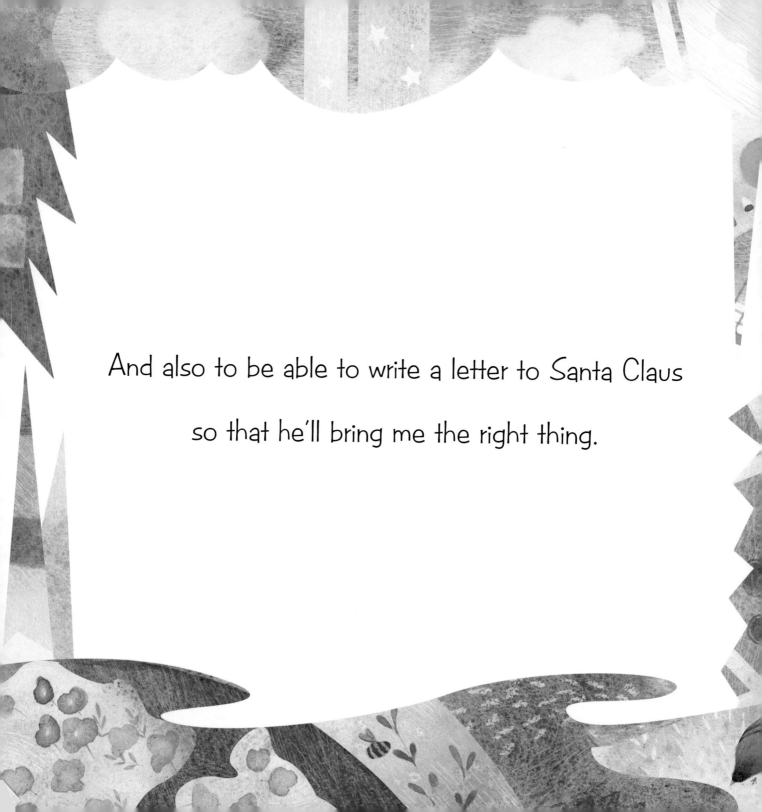

And also to be able to write a letter to Santa Claus

so that he'll bring me the right thing.

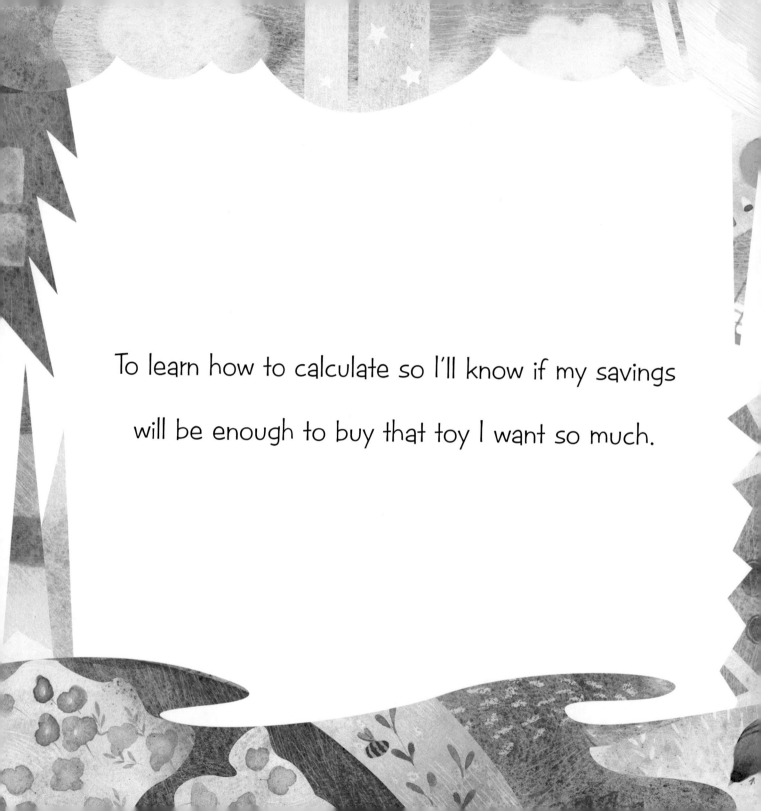

To learn how to calculate so I'll know if my savings

will be enough to buy that toy I want so much.

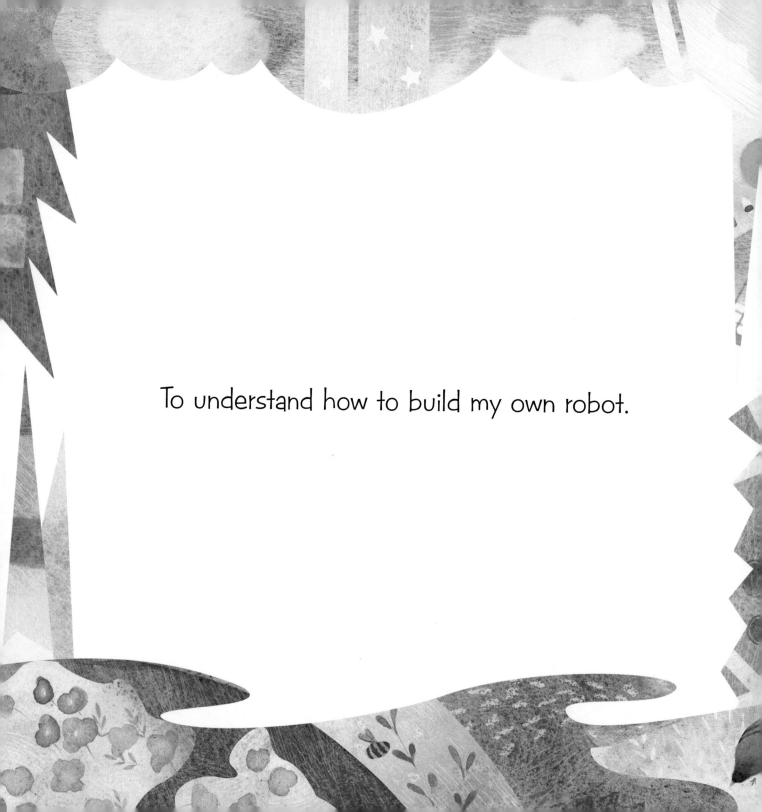

To understand how to build my own robot.

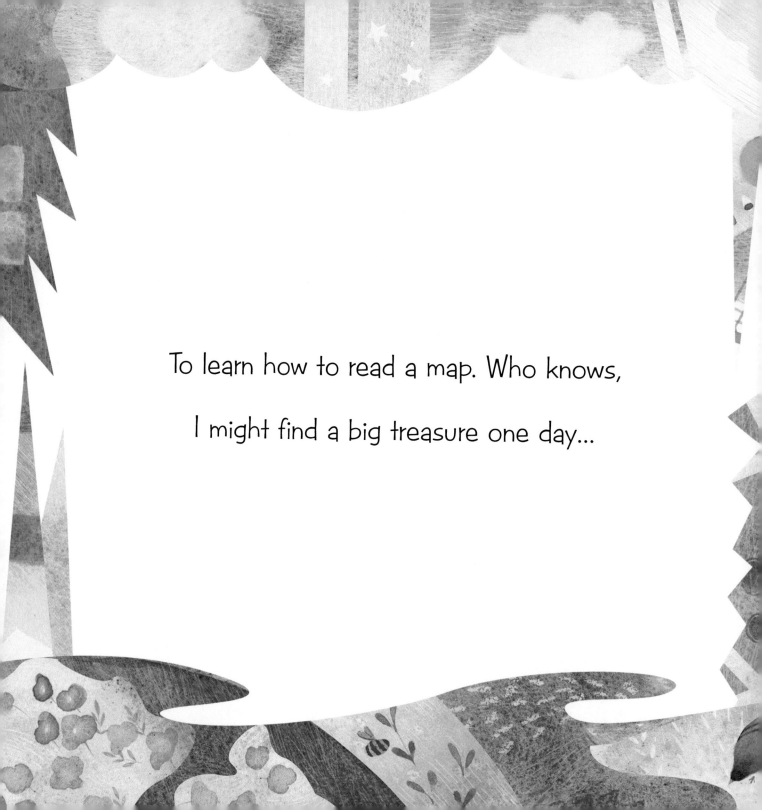

To learn how to read a map. Who knows,

I might find a big treasure one day...

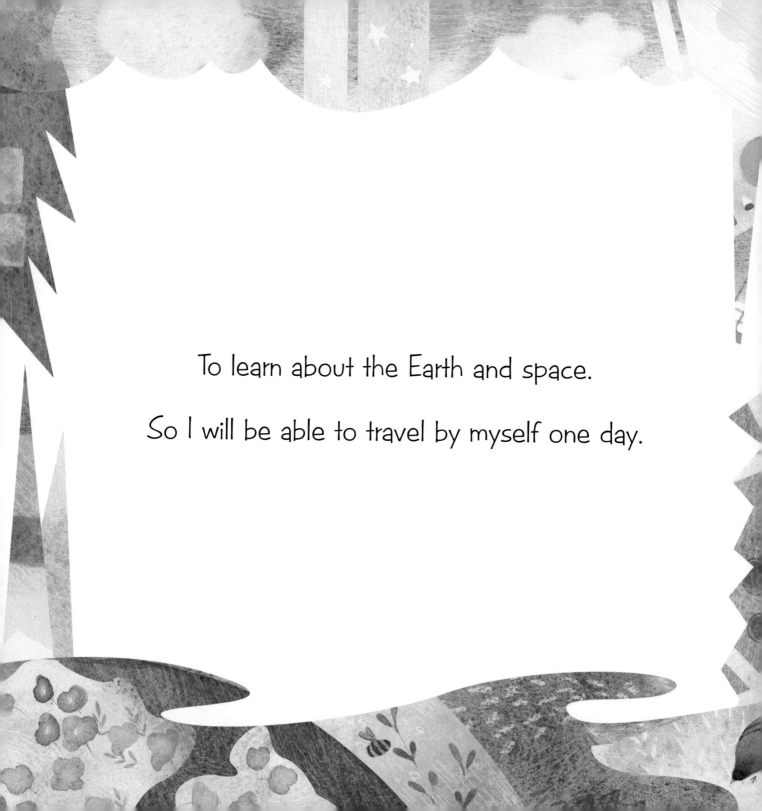

To learn about the Earth and space.

So I will be able to travel by myself one day.

To sum up:

I'll be able to get the things I need

And create new things

Then maybe help other people

And go really, really far.

About the Author

Elise is a Japanese-Brazilian with a bachelor's degree in Portuguese Letters from São Paulo State University, where she studied Brazilian and Portuguese pedagogy, language and literature. She has experience teaching young people and was a researcher in education for foreign children at Kyushu Sangyo University in Japan in 2009. She currently resides in Pittsburgh, USA, where she likes to spend her time with family, friends and books besides learning about different cultures, volunteering and making art.

Printed in the United States
by Baker & Taylor Publisher Services